Hold That Thought!

Written by **BREE GALBRAITH**

Illustrated by **LYNN SCURFIELD**

Owlkids Books

In the middle of the night,
Finn was awakened by something rustling
around inside their head.

It wasn't heavy like a worry,

it didn't swirl like a fear,

and it certainly wasn't shaped
like a question.

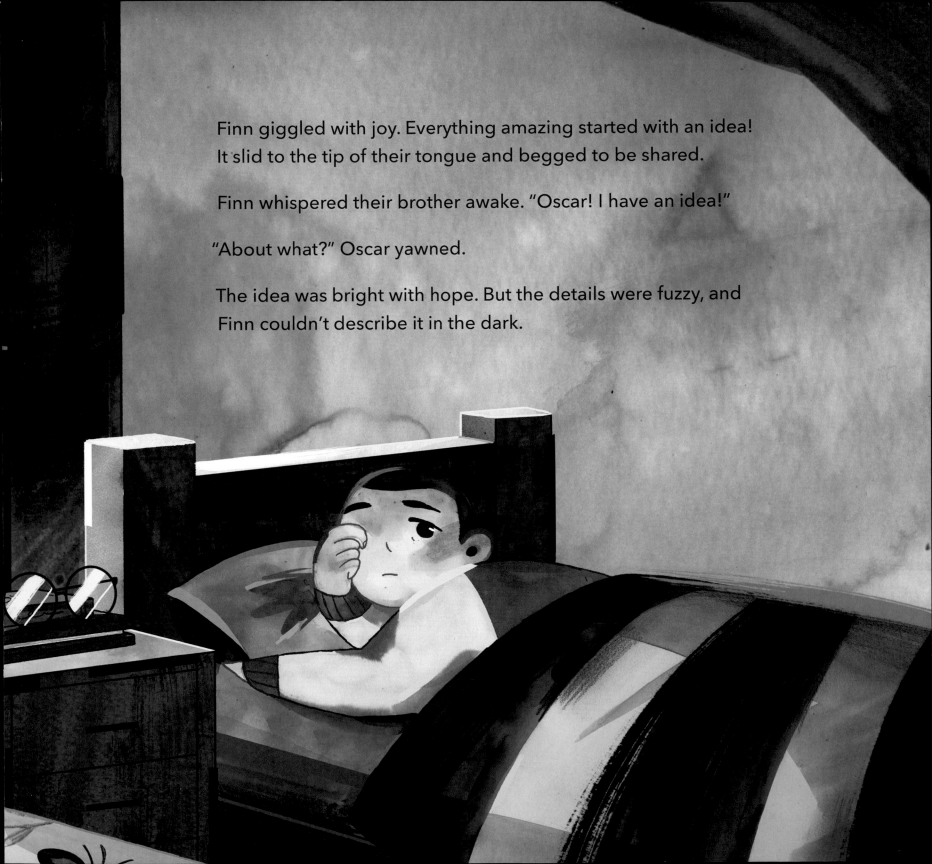

Finn giggled with joy. Everything amazing started with an idea! It slid to the tip of their tongue and begged to be shared.

Finn whispered their brother awake. "Oscar! I have an idea!"

"About what?" Oscar yawned.

The idea was bright with hope. But the details were fuzzy, and Finn couldn't describe it in the dark.

"Hold that thought," whispered Oscar, falling back to sleep. "There's no telling what it could turn into."

And so Finn did. They dreamt about it until morning, when the idea tickled them awake.

On the way to school, the idea sprouted, filling Finn's hand. Finn covered the idea to keep it safe.

When they arrived, Finn hurried to show their best friend.

"Sima! I have the best idea!" Finn said. The idea flew into the air, expanding so quickly, it tumbled backward, sideways, and even a bit upside down.

"I think you're on to something!"
Sima said. "Maybe it needs more
time to come together?"

The friends gathered all the parts,
turned them around, and rolled them
back together until the idea looked
a bit like a plan, sort of like a point …
but mostly like a possibility.

All morning, the idea continued to grow, and Finn's excitement grew right along with it. Eventually, during library time, they had to tuck it up their sleeve to keep it still. Finn's reading buddy, Eleanor, was quick to notice.

"What are you hiding, Finn?" she asked.

"An idea!" Finn exclaimed.

"Shhhhhhhhhh,"

said the librarian.

Eleanor lowered her voice. "I don't think you should hide it," she said. "All good ideas need to be worked out."

Finn peered up their sleeve and invited the idea out with a playful jiggle, and it rolled down, larger than ever.

All afternoon, the idea rumbled around in Finn's desk. Finn could hardly contain it. And they certainly couldn't ignore it. The more Finn thought about it, the bigger and more marvelous it became.

By the end of the day, the idea was so huge that Finn couldn't see over it. So they didn't notice the children gathering around.

Otis knocked the idea out of Finn's arms, and it thumped to the ground.

"What is that weird thing?" he demanded.

"It's not weird," Finn protested. "It's an idea."

"Well, I've never seen one that looks like that!" said Otis, opening his hand.
"Ideas should look like this."

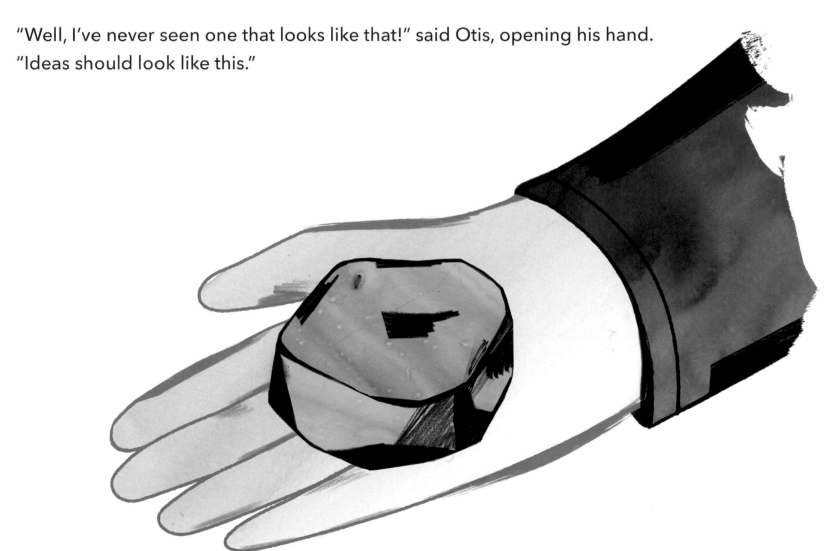

A shadow of doubt crept into Finn's head.
Was there something wrong with their idea?

"You just need to have an open mind," said Finn.
They knelt down and scooped their idea up.
It was cold and still and had lost its glow.

"If your mind is too open," Otis laughed,
"all your thoughts will fall out."

Finn shoved the idea into their pocket. The deeper they buried it, and the more they doubted it, the smaller it became.

Only moments ago, Finn believed their idea was on its way to becoming something spectacular. Now it was only the size of a sparkle.

Finn pulled out the idea and took a closer look. But they saw nothing wrong. The idea was squiggly, rough, notched, soft, sparkly, and ... exactly how it should be?

Exactly how it should be! Finn was sure of it.

Now Finn knew just what to do.
The idea whirled around as they
held it out to the crowd.

Oscar was the first to lend a thought. The idea purred. Next came Sima, and the idea widened. When Eleanor joined in, the idea multiplied. No one knew what they were making, but everyone wanted to be part of it.

Everyone but Otis.

Otis clenched his fist around his idea. He wondered how something so small could feel so heavy. When he turned it over, he felt something spin in his head, and the more he thought about it, the more his idea changed shape.

When he felt like he had something to share, Otis looked to Finn.

Finn beamed as Otis's idea joined the others.

Everything amazing started with an idea, and there was no telling where this one would go!

To all the kids who know that
their ideas won't change the world
unless they share them, this book
is for you — **B.G.**

To all the family, friends, and
teachers I've been lucky enough to
have in my life who have encouraged
me to follow my passions and always
be authentically me — **L.S.**

Owlkids Books acknowledges the financial support of the Canada
Council for the Arts, the Ontario Arts Council, the Government of Canada
through the Canada Book Fund (CBF) and the Government of Ontario
through the Ontario Creates Book Initiative for our publishing activities.

Published in Canada by Owlkids Books Inc.,
1 Eglinton Avenue East, Toronto, ON M4P 3A1

Published in the US by Owlkids Books Inc.,
1700 Fourth Street, Berkeley, CA 94710

Library of Congress Control Number: 2020951495

Library and Archives Canada Cataloguing in Publication

Title: Hold that thought! / written by Bree Galbraith ;
illustrated by Lynn Scurfield.
Names: Galbraith, Bree, author. | Scurfield, Lynn, illustrator.
Identifiers: Canadiana 20200409336 | ISBN 9781771472944 (hardcover)
Classification: LCC PS8613.A4592 H65 2021 | DDC jC813/.6—dc23

The artwork was created with pencil drawings and ink textures that were
scanned and digitally collaged.

Edited by Debbie Rogosin | Designed by Alisa Baldwin

Manufactured in Shenzhen, Guangdong, China, in March 2021, by C&C Offset
Job #HU7851

A   B   C   D   E   F

Publisher of Chirp, Chickadee and OWL | Owlkids Books is a division of bayard canada
www.owlkidsbooks.com